# AN
# AMERICAN
# FACE

BY

## Jan M. Czech

ILLUSTRATED BY

## Frances Clancy

Child and Family Press • Washington, DC

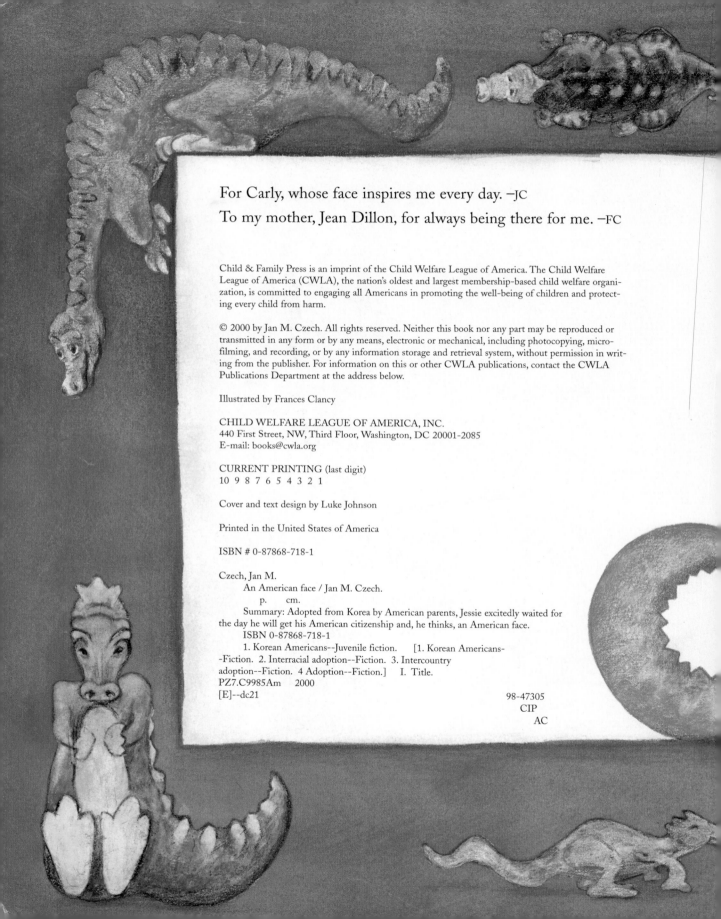

For Carly, whose face inspires me every day. —JC

To my mother, Jean Dillon, for always being there for me. —FC

Child & Family Press is an imprint of the Child Welfare League of America. The Child Welfare League of America (CWLA), the nation's oldest and largest membership-based child welfare organization, is committed to engaging all Americans in promoting the well-being of children and protecting every child from harm.

Illustrated by Frances Clancy

CHILD WELFARE LEAGUE OF AMERICA, INC.
440 First Street, NW, Third Floor, Washington, DC 20001-2085
E-mail: books@cwla.org

CURRENT PRINTING (last digit)
10 9 8 7 6 5 4 3 2 1

Cover and text design by Luke Johnson

Printed in the United States of America

ISBN # 0-87868-718-1

Czech, Jan M.
      An American face / Jan M. Czech.
            p.      cm.
      Summary: Adopted from Korea by American parents, Jessie excitedly waited for the day he will get his American citizenship and, he thinks, an American face.
      ISBN 0-87868-718-1
      1. Korean Americans--Juvenile fiction.      [1. Korean Americans--Fiction. 2. Interracial adoption--Fiction. 3. Intercountry adoption--Fiction. 4 Adoption--Fiction.]      I. Title.
PZ7.C9985Am      2000
[E]--dc21
                                                                98-47305
                                                                   CIP
                                                                    AC

Jessie counted the days until his face would change. Every night he made a big red X through that date on the calendar.

*Ten days to go…*

Each night, before he marked his calendar, he looked in the mirror. This face wasn't an American face. This face had a flat nose. The eyes were slanted instead of round. The skin was light brown. Jessie knew when he got his American face that everything would change.

"Maybe I'll have blue eyes," he said to Chloe, his cat. "Maybe I'll have blond hair. My nose will be longer. Maybe I'll look just like Dad. Or maybe my hair will be curly and brown like Mom's. Maybe I'll have darker skin like my teacher, Ms. Russell."

"Meow-be," said Chloe. She stretched like a rubber band and then curled into a ball on the couch.

*Nine days to go...*

Jessie didn't tell his mom and dad about his face changing. He thought they knew. After all, in eight days he was going to become an American citizen. Jessie figured he couldn't be an American without an American face. He wondered if it would hurt. "Maybe it will feel like when the dentist makes me open my mouth really wide," he said to Chloe. He decided he didn't care if it hurt.

*Eight days...*

When he went to kindergarten, he looked at the kids in his class. They must all be Americans. None of them looked like him. None of them had flat noses and slanted eyes. He wondered if they would recognize him after his face changed.

*Seven days...*

Jessie rode his bike to the park. His mom walked behind him. He looked at all the children playing. A girl with light brown braids and a freckled nose squealed as she slid down the big slide. Two brown-haired boys with holes in the knees of their jeans were swinging. Others dangled from the monkey bars. None of the children looked like him. They had American faces.

*Six days…*

Jessie and his mom went to the grocery store. They bought cornflakes and coffee and his father's favorite cookies. They stood in the express line. Two ladies stood behind them. "You'd think people would take one of their own, instead of adopting

foreigners," one said to the other. Jessie watched his mom turn and glare at the lady. The lady blushed bright red and looked away. Jessie wished he had his American face right now. He wished he didn't look so foreign, so different.

*Five days...*

Jessie's dad worked at the baseball stadium. On Saturday, he took Jessie to a baseball game. "Hot dogs, get your hot dogs here." The hot dog man had eyes like Jessie's. Jessie figured he must not be an American yet, either. The man winked at Jessie. Jessie's dad bought two hot dogs, one for Jessie and one for himself.

*Four days…*

Jessie stayed overnight at his grandma's
house. "This is your great-great-grandpa
when he was a soldier in the Civil War,"
she said, pointing to a picture on the wall.
Jessie giggled, because the man had long,
curly sideburns and a curly mustache.
Jessie hoped he wouldn't look like
that when he got his
American face.

*Three days...*

"We need to get you a suit for your big day," said Jessie's mom. They drove to the mall. Jessie tried on at least one hundred suits. The man in the store wore a turban wrapped around his head. Jessie figured he hadn't gotten his new face yet. Maybe there was a waiting list. After suit one hundred and one, his mom smiled and said, "That's the one for my almost-American-citizen son." The man smiled, too.

*Two days...*

Jessie's class was choosing up teams for soccer.
"You can't play on my team," said Charlie.
"Why not?" Jessie asked.
"Because I don't like the way you look."
Jessie's throat got a lump the size of a baseball.
Tears pressed against his eyelids. He blinked hard so

Charlie wouldn't see him cry. Then he thought, "When my face changes, I won't play on his team, even if he begs me to."

*One day...*

Jessie looked in the bathroom mirror before he went to bed. He stood on the wooden stool under the sink and traced his eyes with his finger. He wrinkled his nose.

"Goodbye, old face," he whispered.

# THE DAY...

Jessie and his mom and dad sat in the crowded courtroom. "Why are there so many people here?" Jessie asked.

"Today they will all become American citizens, just like you, Jessie," said his dad.

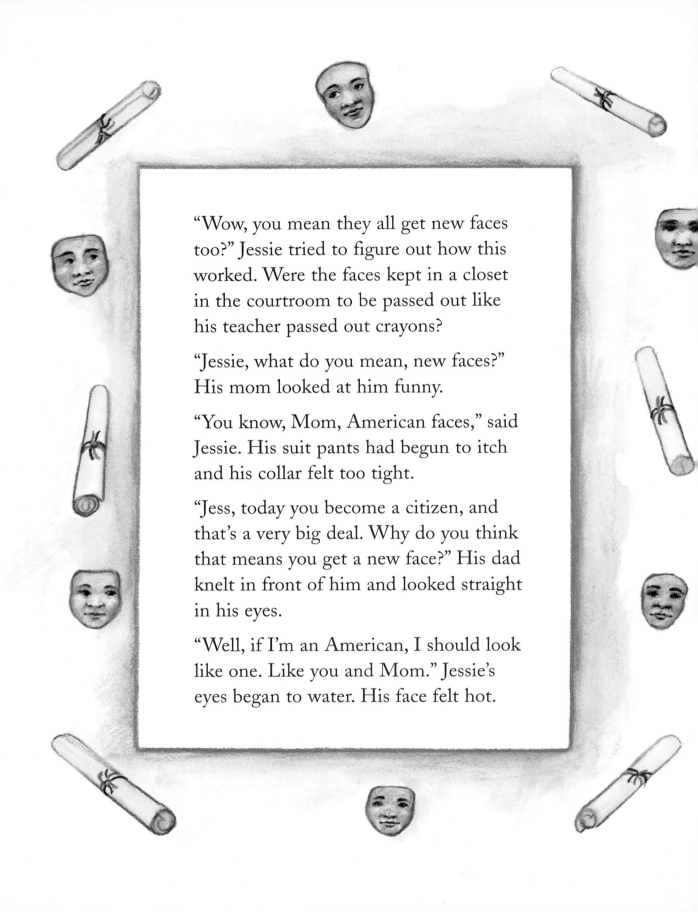

"Wow, you mean they all get new faces too?" Jessie tried to figure out how this worked. Were the faces kept in a closet in the courtroom to be passed out like his teacher passed out crayons?

"Jessie, what do you mean, new faces?" His mom looked at him funny.

"You know, Mom, American faces," said Jessie. His suit pants had begun to itch and his collar felt too tight.

"Jess, today you become a citizen, and that's a very big deal. Why do you think that means you get a new face?" His dad knelt in front of him and looked straight in his eyes.

"Well, if I'm an American, I should look like one. Like you and Mom." Jessie's eyes began to water. His face felt hot.

"Jessie, there are all kinds of ways an American can look. Think about it. How about Mr. Lee, the hot dog man at the ball game? He was born right here. He's an American," said Jessie's dad.

"Yes, Jessie, and Mr. Sandhu, at the clothing store," said Jessie's mom. "He told me he got his citizenship last year."

"You mean, when I become an American, my face won't change so I look like you?"

"No, Jessie. You will always look just like you," said Jessie's mom. She hugged him. Jessie got a knot in his stomach. One tear ran down his face.

"All rise for the Honorable Carolyn Cheung," said a man in front of the courtroom. Everybody stood up. Jessie's dad lifted him so he could see over the heads of the people in front of him. Everyone was quiet. Everyone waited for the judge to speak.

Jessie looked at the judge. Her eyes were slanted. She had a flat nose. Her skin was light brown. All the people in the courtroom were quiet while she spoke. Jessie smiled.

"She looks like me," he said. "Everyone is listening to her."
"That's right," whispered his mom. "She has the second best face in the room."
"Who has the best, Mom?"
"You do, Jessie."

The adults around Jessie were repeating something that the judge had just said. Jessie listened and tried to repeat it too, but before he got the hang of it, the judge stopped.

Jessie's dad handed him a small American flag and said, "Now you have the best American face in the room." Jessie smiled and waved his flag. High on her bench, Judge Cheung smiled too.